William Wobbly

and the Very Bad Day

in the same series

Sophie Spikey Has a Very Big Problem
A story about refusing help and needing to be in control
Sarah Naish and Rosie Jefferies
Illustrated by Amy Farrell
ISBN 978 1 78592 141 4
eISBN 978 1 78450 415 1

Rosie Rudey and the Very Annoying Parent
A story about a prickly child who is scared of getting close
Sarah Naish and Rosie Jefferies
Illustrated by Amy Farrell
ISBN 978 1 78592 150 6
eISBN 978 1 78450 412 0

Charley Chatty and the Wiggly Worry Worm
A story about insecurity and attention-seeking
Sarah Naish and Rosie Jefferies
Illustrated by Amy Farrell
ISBN 978 1 78592 149 0
eISBN 978 1 78450 410 6

William Wobbly

and the Very Bad Day

Sarah Naish and Rosie Jefferies

Illustrated by Amy Farrell

Jessica Kingsley Publishers
London and Philadelphia

First published in 2017
by Jessica Kingsley Publishers
73 Collier Street
London N1 9BE, UK
and
400 Market Street, Suite 400
Philadelphia, PA 19106, USA

www.jkp.com

Copyright © Sarah Naish 2017

Library of Congress Cataloging in Publication Data
A CIP catalog record for this book is available from the Library of Congress

British Library Cataloguing in Publication Data
A CIP catalogue record for this book is available from the British Library

ISBN 978 1 78592 151 3
eISBN 978 1 78450 411 3

Printed and bound in China

Meet William Wobbly and his family

William Wobbly lives with his mum, dad and three sisters, Sophie Spikey, Rosie Rudey and Charley Chatty. The children did not have an easy start in life and now live with their new mum and dad.

All the stories I have written about them are true stories. The children are real children who had difficult times, and were left feeling as if they could not trust grown-ups to sort anything out or look after them properly. Sometimes the children were sad, sometimes very angry. Often they did things which upset other people but they did not understand why.

In this story, William is having a very bad day. He worries about school and losing things and seems to make his mum sigh a lot. William's mum is helping him to make sense of his muddly feelings. Written by William's mum and his sister (who had a lot of wobbly feelings), this story will help everyone feel a bit better.

William Wobbly woke up with that wobbly feeling again.

He didn't know where it came from but he DID know it made his face grumpy, and his head feel very busy.

He didn't want to go to school.

School was SO noisy and made him
feel scared inside.

He tried to tell Mum but she was 'TOO BUSY!'

At breakfast his fingers and feet were all 'tippy tappy'.

Mum looked at them and sighed.

When it was time to go to school, he couldn't find his shoes.

He always lost his shoes.

Mum sighed.

William felt MORE wobbly inside.

On the way to school he wanted to run and run and run.

Mum said, "Hold my hand and walk nicely."

The wobbly feeling got bigger.

He got to school and saw all the children playing with their friends in the school playground.

The wobbly feeling got bigger.

Mum gave him a kiss goodbye and left.

The rushy feeling in his tummy whooshed up into his chest.

The wobbly feeling got so big it went right over his head!

Alfie and Callum came and asked William if he wanted to play football with them.

William couldn't hear them properly because of all the wobbliness, whooshing and rushing noises in his head and ears.

Alfie started laughing.

Suddenly William's arms were hitting Alfie. It was as if the wobbliness had whooshed straight into his arms to make Alfie go away!

Alfie fell over and started crying.

William didn't cry.

The teacher came over with a cross face. She said, "William Wobbly, what on earth do you think you are doing? What an unkind thing to do!"

William felt his whole body go hot. The wobbliness didn't go away. He could see the teacher's mouth moving but couldn't hear what she was saying.

William wanted the hot feeling to go away so his arms pushed the teacher hard. That didn't make the feeling go.

The teacher's mouth made an interesting O shape. William Wobbly wondered what that meant.

The teacher said this was VERY serious. She said she had to phone William's mum RIGHT AWAY!

William had to go to sit on the chairs outside the office.

He knew everyone was staring at him because children only sat on those chairs when something bad had happened.

Mum came in and made a sighing face at him. William felt the wobbliness start off again inside. He didn't want Mum to have a sighing face. He wanted her to smile at him to make the wobbliness go away.

Mum came and sat next to William. She touched his shoulder and said, "I know something has happened. Are you feeling ok?"

William noticed something strange. The whooshing and rushing noises suddenly got smaller.

William managed to do a brave nod.

Mum put her arm round William and said, "I can see you are finding this very difficult. But I know you have a good heart and we can fix this together. I will help you."

William felt his body go all weird and saggy. He leant into Mum and started trying to tell her about the whooshing and the wobbling. He didn't think his words made much sense.

Mum said to him, "When you were a very little boy, before you came to live with me, you couldn't learn to control your wobbly feelings. This wasn't your fault. It was because you didn't have a grown-up helping you to do that. All babies and tiny children need grown-ups to help them sort out wobbly feelings.

Now you are bigger, your wobbly feelings are so big they sometimes burst right out of you, and make you do things you don't want to do.

That's ok though. I know you have a good heart and I am going to help you to be in charge of those wobbly feelings."

The teacher came out with a cross face. William was worried and looked at Mum. She didn't have a sighing face anymore. She didn't look cross either.

Mum held out her hand.

William felt the wobbliness and rushing noises get very, very tiny.

He took Mum's hand and walked into the teacher's office with her.

Later that day, at home, William thought about what Mum had said about the wobbly feelings which hadn't been sorted out when he was very tiny.

Mum had explained to him that there would probably be a lot of days when he felt wobbly as it might take a long time to sort out.

When William was alone in his bed, he remembered his mum saying, "I know you have a good heart."

William fell asleep with a little smile...

...right near the wobbly feeling.

The End

A note for parents and carers, from the authors

This book was written to help you to help your child.

William Wobbly has many of the behavioural and emotional issues experienced by children who have suffered trauma and have attachment difficulties. You will see in this story that William does not understand why he does the things he does and is overwhelmed by feelings, sensory overload and shame. William finds it difficult to communicate his feelings, and to make eye contact and reciprocate physical contact in the illustrations.

We provide training to parents, adopters and foster carers, who have said to us that they often feel out of their depth, and do not know what to say or do when faced with these issues. This story not only gives you valuable insight into *why* our children behave this way, but also enables you to read helpful words, through the therapeutic parent (William's adoptive mum), to your own child.

This story not only names feelings for the child, but also gives parents and carers therapeutic parenting strategies within the story. It features some techniques which you can try in your own family:

- **'Naming the need'** – As parents, we need to be aware of the impact of early life trauma on our children. This trauma is often demonstrated through our children's behaviours. By looking carefully at these behaviours and thinking about where they may have come from, we can relate them to the cause and help the child to make sense of their own thoughts, feelings and behaviours. This is one of the most empowering things we can do as therapeutic parents. The story links William's current angry behaviour to his early life experiences.

- **Using touch to regulate** – Many of our children function at a much younger emotional age, and never learned to control their emotions (self-regulate) as young babies. When our children are very upset, angry or spiralling out of control, simply placing a calm hand on their shoulder can help them to calm and to self-regulate. This kind of touch is not expected to be reciprocated.

- **Telling the child they have a 'good heart'** – When our children show distressing behaviours they are overwhelmed by shame. Early life trauma and neglect have often given our children an internal dialogue which tells them they are 'bad'. Therapeutic parents can empathise with their child and give them an alternative positive view in moments of crisis, by showing the child that they see past their behaviours.

Sarah is a therapeutic parent of five adopted siblings, now all adults, former social worker and owner of an 'Outstanding' therapeutic fostering agency. Rosie is her daughter, and checked and amended William's thoughts and expressed feelings to ensure they are as accurate a reflection as possible. Together, we now spend all our time training and helping parents, carers, social workers and other professionals to heal traumatised children.

Please use this story to make connections, explain behaviours and build attachments between your child and yourself.

Therapeutic parenting makes everything possible.

Warmest regards,

Sarah Naish and Rosie Jefferies

If you liked William Wobbly, why not meet Callum Kindly, Charley Chatty, Katie Careful, Rosie Rudey and Sophie Spikey

---

Callum Kindly and the Very Weird Child

A story about sharing your home with a new child

Rosie Rudey and the Enormous Chocolate Mountain

A story about hunger, overeating and using food for comfort

Charley Chatty and the Disappearing Pennies

A story about lying and stealing

Katie Careful and the Very Sad Smile

A story about anxious and clingy behaviour

William Wobbly and the Mysterious Holey Jumper

A story about fear and coping

Rosie Rudey and the Very Annoying Parent

A story about a prickly child who is scared of getting close

Charley Chatty and the Wiggly Worry Worm

A story about insecurity and attention-seeking

Sophie Spikey Has a Very Big Problem

A story about refusing help and needing to be in control